GOOD NIGHT, FRED

Dial Books for Young Readers

E. P. DUTTON, INC.
New York

GOOD NIGHT,
FRED Rosemary Wells

TO BEEZOO WELLS

Dial Books for Young Readers
A Division of E. P. Dutton, Inc.
2 Park Avenue
New York, New York 10016

GOOD NIGHT, FRED
is published in a hardcover edition by
Dial Books for Young Readers.
ISBN 0-8037-0059-8

The art consists of watercolor paintings, which are
camera-separated and reproduced in full color.

"Stop bouncing, Fred," said Fred's
  brother, Arthur.
"I'm not bouncing," said Fred.

But over he went with the
table and the telephone.

"You did it, Fred," said Arthur.
"The telephone is dead!"
"But Grandma's in the telephone,"
   said Fred. "We just talked to her."

"Don't be silly, Fred," said Arthur.
"There's nothing in here but wires and stuff.
 Now go play with your new tugboat."
"Can you fix the phone, Arthur?" Fred asked.
"Maybe," said Arthur.

Fred did not want to play with his
new tugboat.
"Are you going to tell Mother and
Daddy, Arthur?" he called.
"Maybe," said Arthur.

"Is it going well, Arthur?" Fred asked.
"No," said Arthur. "Go have some
 cake, Fred."
"I'll get you a nice big piece," said Fred.

"I brought you a piece with a rose,"
  said Fred.
"Later, Fred," said Arthur.
"Are you sure Grandma's not in there?"
  Fred asked.

"Grandma lives hundreds and hundreds of
  miles away, Fred," said Arthur.
"Now, go to bed."
"Will you kiss me good night, Arthur?"
  asked Fred.
"Yes!" said Arthur.

"Arthur," said Fred, "we forgot the
Good Night, Fred Song."
"I'll sing it from down here,"
said Arthur.

Fred could not sleep.
He could not hear Arthur.

"Arthur!" he shouted.
Arthur did not answer.
Fred fell out of bed.

Bang! went Fred on the floor.
Arthur did not come.

Fred went down the stairs.
"Arthur?" he called.

Arthur was not there.
"I'm all alone!" said Fred.

Suddenly the telephone rang.

"Hello," said Fred. "Who is it,
    please?"
"It's me," said Grandma, "and I'm
    coming out."

"I knew you were in there,"
said Fred.
"Of course!" said Grandma.

"Are you hungry?" asked Fred.
"I'd love a piece of cake," said
Grandma.

"Would you like to have some fun?"
  Fred asked.
"I'd love to have some fun,"
  said Grandma.

So Fred gave Grandma a tugboat ride.

Then Grandma taught Fred some of
the songs she sang when she was a girl.

Then they bounced

and bounced

and bounced until it was time for
Grandma to go home.
"Good night, Fred," said Grandma.

And she kissed him and tucked
him in, and Fred slept.

Until Arthur came back.
"Where were you?" Fred asked.
"In the garage," said Arthur,
"looking for the saw."

"But the telephone's fixed
  now," said Fred.
"It is?" said Arthur.
"Grandma called," said Fred.
"She did?" said Arthur.

"Now would you sing the Good Night,
Fred Song, Arthur?" Fred asked.
"Yes," said Arthur, and he sang all
the verses.